Jack of All Tails

by Kim Norman

illustrated by David Clark

DUTTON CHILDREN'S BOOKS

DUTTON CHILDREN'S BOOKS
A division of Penguin Young Readers Group

Published by the Penguin Group

Penguin Group (USA) Inc., 375 Hudson Street, New York, New York 10014, U.S.A. • Penguin Group (Canada), 90 Eglinton Avenue East, Suite 700, Toronto, Ontario,
Canada M4P 2Y3 (a division of Pearson Penguin Canada Inc.) • Penguin Books Ltd, 80 Strand, London WC2R 0RL, England • Penguin Ireland, 25 St Stephen's Green,
Dublin 2, Ireland (a division of Penguin Books Ltd) • Penguin Group (Australia), 250 Camberwell Road, Camberwell, Victoria 3124, Australia (a division of Pearson
Australia Group Pty Ltd) • Penguin Books India Pvt Ltd, 11 Community Centre, Panchsheel Park, New Delhi-110 017, India • Penguin Group (NZ), Cnr Airborne and
Rosedale Roads, Albany, Auckland 1310, New Zealand (a division of Pearson New Zealand Ltd) • Penguin Books (South Africa) (Pty) Ltd, 24 Sturdee Avenue, Rosebank,
Johannesburg 2196, South Africa • Penguin Books Ltd, Registered Offices: 80 Strand, London WC2R 0RL, England

LIBRARY OF CONGRESS CATALOGING-IN-PUBLICATION DATA
Norman, Kimberly.
Jack of All Tails / by Kim Norman—illustrated by David Clark.—1st ed.
p. cm.
Summary: Members of the Kibbleman family take on jobs training people to live with their pets,
wallowing in mud like the Munsons' pot-bellied pig or lying in front of the television and passing gas
like Mrs. Philpott's dearly departed boxer dog, MacTavish.
ISBN 978-0-525-47793-8 (hardcover-alk. paper) [1. Pets—Fiction. 2. Business enterprises—Fiction. 3. Humorous stories—Fiction.]
I. Clark, David (David Lynn), date, ill. II. Title.
PZ7.N7846Jac 2007
[E]—dc22   2006024784

Published in the United States by Dutton Children's Books,
a division of Penguin Young Readers Group
345 Hudson Street, New York, New York 10014
www.penguin.com/youngreaders

Designed by Jason Henry
Manufactured in China • First Edition
1 3 5 7 9 10 8 6 4 2

For my parents, who filled my childhood
with books and weird pets
—KN

To the Family,
my bunch of animals
—DG

My family is a bunch of animals...for the right price. We snuffle and snuggle and snort for a living.

It all started when Pickles had puppies. Pickles is the bulldog who lives with the Deener family.

One day, I heard Mrs. Deener say to my dad, "I don't know a thing about puppies!"

"Oh, let us help! We're good with animals!" I said.

Later, Dad asked me, "Why did you say that, Kristi? We don't even own a pet!"

"Sorry," I said. "The puppies were so cute, I got carried away."

"Cute puppies or not, try to slow down and think first," Dad said.

But we did help. Since the puppies were too little to play, we showed
the Deener kids what would happen when the puppies got older.
My brother, Eddie, fetched a tennis ball.

Mom played tug-of-war with an old sock.
Dad did tricks, like rolling over and begging.

With a squirt bottle, I taught the kids about puppy puddles.
Then I chewed up Ralphie Deener's spelling list.

"No, no! Bad puppy!" said Mrs. Deener.
Too late. I'd eaten every word except "buttress."

"It was kind of fun acting like a dog today," Eddie said at dinner that night.

"Yes, I think Kristi was right. We are good with animals," said Dad.

"I have another idea," I offered.

"Uh-oh. What have you cooked up now?" Mom asked.

So I told them my idea for a family business. "We can be people trainers—you know, teach them how to take care of their pets."

My parents looked at each other. "Maybe it would work," said Mom.

"I guess we could try it on the side," said Dad.

"It's okay with me, as long as it pays," said Eddie.

It didn't take long for word to spread about our new company.
I put an ad on the back of my jacket. That, along with some posters,
a website, and a sign on our van, did the trick.

Our first paying customers were the McGinn family. They adopted a cat from the animal shelter. "Can you help my daughter with her new kitty the way you helped the Deener children?" Mr. McGinn asked. So we did.

Eddie chased a marble under the sofa.

Mom pounced on a string.
Dad flopped down in a sunny spot to nap.

I showed how frisky a cat can be. I frolicked
around legs and lamps and chewed on spider plants.
"No, no! Bad kitty!" said Mr. McGinn.
Too late. I'd already pulled down the drapes.

At home, Mom swabbed my skinned knee and said, "Maybe you need to learn more about animals, Kristi." What a great idea! I sat in the vet's office for an hour, studying the pets in the waiting room. They seemed tense.

Next, I visited the zoo. Even though no one is likely to hire me as a hippo, I can do a great roar. I spent a long time watching the monkeys. By the end of the day, I could spit a peanut over a whole class of second graders.

HIPPO POND

MONKEYS

A few days later, Bubba Schwartz hired Eddie and me as lizards. Bubba wanted to prove to his parents that he was old enough to take care of a pet.

Eddie was a great lizard, napping under the sun lamp.

Bubba yelled at me at feeding time, though. "No, no!
Bad lizard!" he said.
   Too late. In one gulp, I'd eaten a week's worth of crickets.

Things hadn't exactly been going my way (people were hard to train!), so I was a little nervous the first time I worked alone. The Munson family hired me to stand in for Jelly Bean, their pot-bellied pig. Jelly Bean was little Charlotte Munson's special friend.

When the Munsons sent Jelly Bean away to live on a farm, Charlotte pitched a fit. So they hired me to play dress-up, like Jelly Bean used to do. When Charlotte served tea, I ate all the peanuts... and the poppy seed scones...and the cucumber sandwiches.

After that I felt a little sick, so Charlotte said,
"Come on, Jelly Bean. You're going outside."

Like a good pig, I wallowed in mud before I came back into the house.

"No, no! Bad pig!" scolded Mrs. Munson.
Too late, I found out that Jelly Bean never made a pig of himself,
and he never, ever wallowed in mud. The Munsons did not ask me back.

Now everyone has found permanent work but me. Dad has a steady job working for Mrs. Philpott. She hired him to take the place of her dearly departed boxer dog, MacTavish. After dinner, Mrs. Philpott claps her hands and says, "Time for our game shows, Mackie!" Then Dad does MacTavish's evening job—lying in front of the TV, passing gas during commercials.

Mom fills in for cats like mean old Rosco, who spent his whole life on Mr. Osawa's piano. Rosco was not a music lover. Mom spends the day curled up on a lace doily, swatting at anyone who touches the piano keys.

Even Eddie stays busy doing reptile jobs after school. Well, maybe "busy" isn't the right word. All he does is lie under a heat lamp, munching turtle pellets. Anybody can do that.

When Dad came home from work last week, I helped him unload the van.

"I'm not good at anything!" I said. "I'm a poor puppy, a crummy cat, a lousy lizard, and a perfectly pitiful pig!"

Dad laughed. "You're not bad at those things, Kristi. You're just a bit too eager. You need to find a way to use all that energy with your own special talents."

The next day, I went for a jog.
I thought and I ran. I ran and I thought.

Then it came to me. The perfect job.
So now I'm in training. I know I've got the talent...

It runs in the family!